GRACE

OVER

FEAR

Written and Illustrated by
Bethany L. Correia

A Novel based on a true story.
Based on real events, and real people.
However, names and identifying details
have been changed for the privacy of
Individuals, businesses, and some places.

ISBN 978-1-0980-2861-9 (paperback)
ISBN 978-1-0980-2863-3 (hardcover)
ISBN 978-1-0980-2862-6 (digital)

Christian Faith Publishing, Inc.
832 Park Avenue
Meadville, PA 16335
www.christianfaithpublishing.com

Printed in the United States of America

Contents

Chapter 1

Fear's Probing

She walked through the front door of her home on a Wednesday afternoon and locked it behind her. Grace Jensen plopped down on the couch and placed her bookbag on the ground next to her feet. It was a cool mid-fifty-degree day, but nothing unusual for winter afternoon weather in the southern town of Arizona, Sierra Vista. *Now what?* She sighed. *No time for sitting.* She had homework to do. Grace breathed in deeply, snatched her bag up, and rummaged through the books and papers that were shoved into it as she drudged toward her bedroom. She felt the one-and-a half-inch-thick math book, grabbed it, and slid it out, and then dropped the rest near her closet. She gathered her materials and laid them on the bed, but first she had to get something to eat; her stomach growled at her. Grace went back into the kitchen of her small trailer home, rummaged through the refrigerator, and didn't find anything. So she grabbed an orange from the bowl on the counter. After she ate it, she went to wash her hands to get the sticky juice off. It was then when she heard through the small single-paned kitchen window a man's voice: "Stay there, Rocky."

What in the world? Grace wondered. *Who the heck knows my dog's name? Maybe it's Judah.* Judah was Grace's big brother, who already hit puberty, and his voice recently deepened to a mannish tone. *It's too early for him to get home.*

She dried her hands and went back to business, math homework on the bed. She lay down on her stomach and opened the book to the page marked by a folded piece of paper, her homework already started. She took her pencil and started working. Her mind, however, was not settled. She kept wondering when Judah was going to come in. *Why didn't he come in yet? Maybe he did, and I just didn't hear him.* She paused her pencil to listen a little closer without the extra noise that came from writing. No sounds, quiet. She breathed out because she was holding her breath so she could listen better and started writing again. After writing the rest of the problem down on her lined paper, she suddenly put her pencil down, got up, and went through the whole house.

Where is he? He's not in his room or anywhere else! Maybe he hasn't come in yet. She looked out the window to see if she could spot him. Nope, just Rocky Raccoon, her big pure-bred Akita dog on the chain who was lying under the shade of the large mesquite tree, panting. She shrugged it off and thought her brother must be outside somewhere else, just hadn't come in yet. Back again to finish the problem she started. She lay there, pencil moving.

Step, step, step—dirt and twigs rustled under what sounded like footsteps in front of her, right outside her bedroom window. Grace's pencil froze, and she held her breath for a moment. *Was that real? Or was that my imagination? Who knows… Judah? Not coming in. Hmmm.*

Grace drew in a large breath, shook her head, and continued homework problems. It wasn't a thought, but she felt a wonder in her spirit, whether she should be worried about all this. It was like Fear was pounding on the door of her heart through the perceived sounds of footsteps outside her bedroom window.

Step…step…step…step—again, pencil stopped, breath slowed, quiet as could be, she listened harder. *What in the world? Is this my imagination? Psyching myself out?* Grace's heart started to pound, and suddenly that's all she heard, which also echoed in her mind, like the steps she heard outside her window. Was it real? She couldn't discern reality from imagination anymore. She was getting frustrated

and tense, fretful, trying to sort out the compounded experiences in just that short time of being home.

RINGGGGG!

The sound of the telephone was amplified and startled her immensely. She jumped and thought her heart was going to leap out of her chest. *Okay, Grace, just chill out! It's probably Mom.* "Hello," Grace answered the phone, still a nervous wreck, though she tried to hide it when answering the phone.

"Grace?" It was her mom's voice.

She felt somewhat relieved. "Yes."

"Just checking in on you. Making sure you got home okay."

"Yeah, I'm home. Hey, Mom! I need to tell you something." Grace's heart started racing again. She felt her face flush and heated red with nerves and, well…fear. "When I got home today, I was at the kitchen window, and I heard a man's voice say, 'Stay there, Rocky.' Strange thing. Rocky didn't bark, so I thought it was Judah, but he didn't come in. Then when I was doing my homework on my bed, I thought I heard footsteps outside my window. But I'm not sure if I heard it or if it was my imagination." She had to tell her that part because she just didn't know.

"No, Judah is working with me today. It wasn't Judah. Anthony is with me too. Okay, I'm finishing up with my work. I'll be home in about thirty minutes, okay? Give me a call if you have to though," Grace's mom, Joy Jensen, replied. She sounded like she was going to make haste to come home faster than she originally intended.

"Okay, Mom, see you in a little bit. I'll call you if I need to."

"Okay, Grace, I'll be home in a little bit. I love you."

Grace didn't like saying those words; it always felt awkward to her. But this time, she felt the need to say it back, and she did. Grace hung up the phone.

Making haste, Grace went around to make sure all the doors were locked and shut all the windows and blinds to hide from anyone (if there was anyone), just in case. Heart still pounding, she thought she would feel better knowing her mom would be home soon and that she completed the task of shutting herself inside the trailer from the view of the outside. Whatever she tried in the physical realm to ease her mind didn't work. She was unsuccessful in turning off the pushy thoughts. Those thoughts that incited within her heart and soul were of Fear. She went back to her math work and periodically repeated the pausing of the pencil and holding her breath, only to listen when she thought she heard any little thing.

Grace couldn't help herself. She heard nothing certain but faint noises only when she wrote. *Is it my pencil? Is he only walking when I write? Can he see me? Why would anyone be in our yard? Is someone going to hurt me or come into my house?* Fear probed her mind with unrelenting, pervasive thoughts. How was Grace going to respond? Nothing she did helped. Her heart didn't slow. For all she knew, the "steps" might have been only in her mind. *My mom will be home soon.* She tried to dwell on that thought. It wasn't fun to be home alone with Fear as a twelve-year-old girl. She still wondered who that man's voice belonged to, the one talking to her dog by name—that was one thing she was certain she heard. Fear wasn't even an inkling at the time, so there was no reason for her to hallucinate the voice. Her thoughts grasped for answers some more. *Something's up. What man knows my dog by name? Rocky didn't bark. That means my dog felt comfortable with this man. What man made friends with my dog? It's not my dad. He's in Oregon* [Grace's mom and dad were separated and about to be divorced at the time], *and Judah was with Mom, so it wasn't him.* She searched her mind to try and see if she could think of any other man who knew Rocky. *Maybe the neighbor across the road knew his name.* She didn't know; they were not friends with that neighbor, or any other neighbor for that matter. Grace was able to finish up her math homework, even through the flood of fearful thoughts. She knew math like she knew the back of her hand and was able to complete it thoughtlessly and effortlessly.

Grace sat in the large leather chair in the living room. It was on the same wall as the only window in there. *If I sit here and someone looks through the cracks of the blinds, he, or they, won't be able to see me around the corner.* That's what Grace thought anyway. She was counting down the minutes her mom said she would be home by. It wasn't long when Joy, Judah, and Anthony walked through the door. Everything was going to be okay. Grace could breathe again. Her heart slowed, and she was settled in heart and mind. Grace retold the story to her mom. Before the end of the conversation, Joy said she was going to pray and ask God what all this was and seek answers. Grace didn't think much of it. That night, she slept soundly. All seemed well.

Chapter 2

Grace's Family Background

Grace's life was far from perfect. Maybe from the outside looking in, people may have felt sorry for her and her family. Grace wouldn't have known, but it also didn't cross her mind to even care. They were living off Joy's income, who was a self-employed housecleaner, on welfare and used food stamps. Grace knew she wasn't rich and didn't have the means to get name-brand clothing, shoes, bookbags, etc. Secretly, she'd thought about wearing what everyone at school was wearing as a seventh grader in middle school so as to not be looked at as poor by other students or to just fit in. Ultimately, she couldn't care less. She'd learned to shrug at it, wear what she liked, and be happy to be herself.

Joy and her husband, Allen, have been separated for quite some time, and there was talk of divorce. That didn't surprise Grace one bit. Allen had been in Oregon for the time of the separation. He didn't come around much, or at all really. Allen wasn't much for traveling unless he had to. Grace didn't even know where he was staying in Oregon, but he stayed away. She didn't carry any ill feelings toward her dad. All her life, her parents were either together with much strife or just separated. She didn't know any different and even felt indifferent toward her dad being gone and the talk of divorce. She knew her dad, Allen, didn't and wouldn't step foot in a church door. He had been hurt by the church in the past. He decided to walk away and hadn't been back since. He was mostly an absent father, a workaholic, and an alcoholic too. The majority of his day was spent at work and then the bar and then, if he wasn't asleep, in front of the television. He worked in construction, more specifically drywall. Interaction wasn't really a negative experience with her and her dad. When Grace was little at nighttime, she would sit under his arm in his recliner and watch action movies. He didn't make her do any chores, though Joy would ask her to. Grace didn't have to do them according to dad, and she liked that.

There were times when Joy would have to pick Allen up from the bar late at night because he was too drunk to drive himself. Many times, Grace, Judah, and Anthony, their little brother, would approach the outside bar window, knock on it to get their dad's attention, letting him know the ride, Joy, was here. That was embarrassing. There were times Joy refused to pick him up, so he would walk home. Grace remembered a time when they lived in Oregon. He walked home in the snow late at night, and he looked as if he could have died from the cold. Joy was worried about him and covered him up to regain some warmth. He instantly passed out on the couch.

Once, Grace recalled him coming home slobbering, stumbling drunk. He went to use the restroom and was in there for a long time. Joy checked up on him and found him bent in half, sitting on the toilet, asleep, his pants down and a lit cigarette in his hand, which had burnt a hole in the linoleum floor. Joy was sure not to talk bad about him, whether he was with them or not. But she did use those examples to show her kids that this was something they shouldn't do (get drunk), and she added in the dangers of cigarette smoking too. Grace knew Joy was frustrated with his lifestyle, but she still loved him, even when he was gone. This helped Grace have no ill feelings toward him and no temptation for drugs, cigarettes, or alcohol. Grace saw what it did to a man.

For the most part, Grace formed her thoughts and opinions about both her parents based off who they were and what they did.

Grace was most comfortable living with her mom. Joy Jensen was a hard worker, caring, and did well with what she had. She never let on that there were any financial troubles or difficulties. She worked without complaint. She, a Christian woman, was friendly to everyone, loved meeting new people everywhere she went. Though not rich, she was the most giving and generous of persons. She had this one earthly desire though. She had an intense curiosity to know the future, her future mostly. The future always intrigued her. Bible revelation and prophecy didn't seem adequate to her; maybe she was just ignorant of it. It showed especially when she had unanswered questions about her own personal problems or problems of loved ones. She didn't just seek God for answers, but it was a temptation to gain insights from any source she found, Christian or not. Most important to Grace, though: Joy was faithful in going to church. Attendance was at least three times a week.

They (Joy, Judah, Anthony, and Grace) went to Abundant Life Christian Fellowship at the time of the incident with a man's voice calling to Rocky. They went once on Wednesday evenings and twice on Sundays (a morning and an evening service). That's something Grace felt was a constant in her life, and in her heart it was good and right. Grace knew she could, and did, believe the things she learned at church, everything in the Bible (or what she learned was in the Bible). This included knowledge that Jesus died on the cross to pay for sins, that Jesus rose from the dead three days later, conquering sin and death. When one believed this, they would have eternal life with God, as opposed to dying in sin to suffer eternal damnation in hell. According to the Bible, because she heard and believed these things about Jesus, she was saved, a Christian. As far as she remembered, she always believed these things. Churchgoing was a highlight in Grace's life and her weekly schedule. She had a few friends at church, and they usually sat all together with one of the families and sometimes were allowed to sit together by themselves as long as they were not being disruptive.

Even though Grace loved to be at church, this is the place Fear stealthily snuck his little face in a door and eventually found its way into the Jensen home and into the heart and mind of Grace. However, Fear hid himself until the time was ripe.

Joy and Grace, as with any and all Christians, were ever learning and growing at their individual rates. They struggled with their individual human desires, still got tempted, still slipped up, and still experienced trials and tribulations. They suffered earthly consequences of their own sins and sins of others. They were secure in belief that God was, is, and always will be sovereign and in control over all things. Joy's and Grace's, though not perfected yet, hearts were made new, no longer slaves to sin, able to exercise the commands of God. They've become clean, forgiven, and justified and were securely placed in God's family. God fathered, disciplined, cleansed, taught, comforted, and led them into sanctification. Sanctification was done along in their journeys. It was a process, a walk that would last until they pass into eternal life.

Judah, on the other hand, kept to his own interests. He came to church begrudgingly but tolerated it because he was allowed to sit in the back with his friends during the services. At other times, he was allowed to stay home instead. What he did with his time wasn't really known to Grace as he often went out with his friends who lived around the neighborhood. They roamed the area or hung out outside most of the time. He wasn't involved in the family affairs but enjoyed his time away from home.

Anthony was the youngest sibling. He was a little less than two years younger than Grace, about to be eleven years old. His life revolved around what everyone did as a family. He had a particularly difficult time at school. Fifth grade was the worst for him in Sierra Vista. The kids were very mean to him; they would make fun of him and bully him. He despised going to school because of that. Eventually, Anthony refused to go to school, and there was no way Joy was able to make him. He was very stubborn in that respect, and physically she couldn't pick him up or make him do anything, even though she tried. Joy decided to homeschool for a little bit. Anthony was still reluctant with the work, but he stayed home and went to work with Joy so she could keep an eye on him. Eventually, Anthony decided that when Joy and Allen's divorce was finalized, he was going to move with Allen to Oregon for the school year and stay with Joy over the summers. This was his way of escaping and removing himself from the hostile environments and the people that hurt him.

Chapter 3

Months Leading Up to the Instance

So it happened. On one of the Sunday morning services, a new lady showed up with two of her teenage sons. Abundant Life Christian Fellowship, the church the Jensens attended at the time, wasn't that big, so it was easy to recognize newcomers. This lady was five foot tall. An obese lady with thin straight blonde hair. Her sons were both over six feet tall and also obese. They were closer to Judah's age, who was fifteen at the time. Both boys had curly brown hair. Joy, eager to welcome newcomers as she always did, introduced herself to the new family in the Abundant Life church. Her name was Jean, and her sons' names were Ben, who was sixteen years old, and John, who was eighteen. The greeting time was never that long, so that was as far as they got in introductions. After service, Joy made sure she approached them again to get to know them more and made them feel welcome in the church.

Jean and her boys started coming regularly to every service Abundant Life held. She started to gain a good rapport among the believers. Joy kept approaching the new family and learned a lot about them. As she befriended them more, Jean revealed that she was a witch. She had come from a line of witches and claimed to want to get out of it. That's why she was coming to the Christian church: to "learn" about Christianity and God. Joy took that as a personal challenge or assignment to keep talking with Jean about Jesus. Her hopes were to try to keep them coming to church so maybe they would get saved. In the back of Joy's mind, however, lurked that natural disposition, the curiosity about telling the future. She made a subconscious mental note that that could also be one of Jean's, the witch's, so-called abilities.

Joy, after learning the fact about Jean and her boys, told Judah, Grace, and Anthony, "I was talking with Jean today. Jean said that she and her boys are a witch and warlocks. She said that they were coming to church so they could learn about God and Christianity. She said that because they were born into it, that it is too difficult and dangerous for them to get out. I might try to talk with Jean more. If she's wanting to learn more about God, I would like to keep sharing the Gospel with her. Maybe God would use me to bring her to Jesus, and she would get saved. I was thinking that we could do a get-together with them sometime."

Eventually, Jean had invited the Jensens over for lunch on a Sunday, after morning church. When the time came, Joy, Judah, Grace, and Anthony went to Jean's home. It was at a trailer park in the bad part of the town. Definitely not fancy. Several trailers had junk on their lot, and most of them were poorly kept. All the trailers were lined up in tightly packed rows. Hers was one of the smaller single-wides, closely wedged between a couple other trailers.

Grace felt uneasy being there. Her face made a grimace that she was unaware of, even though she determined to be polite no matter what. Grace herself lived in a trailer;

that wasn't the problem. She wasn't used to that type of environment or neighborhood and didn't want to be around these specific people who claimed to be a part of witchcraft. She didn't have a choice though. Her spirit didn't feel right and felt a heavy wariness in her chest—especially knowing the information her mom found out about this family a couple weeks prior to the visit. Ben and John were there at the door to greet, and Jean had stepped outside to welcome them and led them inside. The boys towered over her petite body when she came through the door and crossed paths, almost touching just to get by. The space was awkwardly tight. Grace squeezed her body together just to not touch. As she crouched by these acquaintances, her space felt violated. She wanted to go, and go now, like she was trapped. *Why didn't I ask Mom if I could stay home?* She felt regret. Grace wasn't usually this uncomfortable, but this was most unpleasant in multiple dimensions—soul, spirit, and body. She did manage to put on a small smile when they were greeted at the door, though she didn't feel like it. In the small cluttered, encroached space of the home, being that Jean and her boys were all obese, she felt physically stuck, and the space started to envelope her. Her face blanked out, trying not to show discomfort.

"Sorry that there's nowhere to really sit. We're just moving in, and we haven't unpacked everything," Jean apologized.

To add to it, there were no couches or furniture to sit on, just one small table with only four chairs in the tiny overcrowded kitchen, where Jean was preparing to serve the meal. Grace tried to disappear into any space that was semiunoccupied when she finally found a stool that wasn't

18

being used. She moved it away from everyone as far as she could and took her permanent seat for the remainder of the visit. All she wanted was for it to be over. As she sat there, trying to eat, though not really hungry anymore, her stomach churned inside. Her focus was to avoid interaction with anyone. *Come on, time, hurry up so we can leave to get ready for evening service.* Grace didn't notice, but her knees started bouncing impatiently.

The boys all headed outside to hang out. They must have felt the cramp and wanted some moving and breathing space, leaving the gals inside. It brought in a little more breathing room, so Grace was able to relax a little more, still hoping and praying that time would go by quickly. The whole time, she just felt yucky inside. It felt like a heaviness, a wariness in her spirit, a rotten weight in her chest. It was spiritually dark and hard to explain. She was ready to leave no later than the time they arrived.

From the physical sense, nothing bad happened. Yet her spirit waved red flags. She had a gut feeling that something was bad.

Finally, the time came to leave, to go get ready for the second church service that day. All eased up again. She soon forgot all the discomforts of the visit.

The Jensens didn't gather together with Jean's family after that, but Joy certainly kept in touch with Jean, all for the purpose to win her soul and be her friend. Jean, Ben, and John continued to attend Abundant Life Christian Fellowship.

Two weeks before Grace experienced hearing that man, whoever he was, talk to her dog through the kitchen window, she had another family dilemma. Joy told the three siblings that she and Allen were getting the divorce and when it would be finalized. In about three weeks, Allen was going to drive down to Sierra Vista to pick up the boys and take them to Oregon with him for the rest of the school year. That's what both Judah and Anthony wanted. Joy and Allen knew their children (Judah, Grace, and Anthony) were old enough to decide whom they wanted to say with over the school year. And of course, they would be with the other parent during the summer. Grace chose to be with her mom during the school year and her dad during the summer. She knew her mom would take her to church, and that was important to her. That, and she didn't really want to change schools again.

Chapter 4

An Answer to "Who"

Friday came. Two days had passed from Fear's probing encounter. It was five thirty in the morning and dark outside. Grace was about to head out the door, ready to catch her school bus. She stuck her head in her mother's room and said, "Bye, Mom, I'm leaving for the bus now."

Her mother responded differently this time, "Hey, Grace, I'm going with you. Hold on, let me get my shoes on. I'm going to walk you to the bus from now on."

"Why, Mom?" Grace argued. "That's embarrassing."

"Just for safety. I want to watch you to make sure you get on the bus."

"I always go to the bus by myself. Why are you going now?" Grace protested, unaware that this was related to the voice she heard Wednesday afternoon two days earlier.

Joy took in a deep breath and told Grace to sit on the bed. "I'm going to tell you something." Grace sat on the opposite side of the bed, and her mom continued, "I asked Jean about what you heard."

Are you serious, Mom? You know she's a witch. She's not going to tell you what God says. Grace prepared herself not to receive anything she (Jean) said.

Joy kept going, "She said that someone was watching you. They are planning to kidnap you, and would hide you in a cellar with dirt floors, cedar steps, and cedar walls. She said that they planned to rape you and then kill you on the third day."

At those words, Grace's body tensed up so tight that she started to literally shake and tremble.

"So that's why you want to go with me to the bus stop?" Grace understood now.

Joy nodded her head. "I asked her more questions to get more information on who. She told me that the man had either an old blue truck or a gray one and lived near us." There was no more information that Joy knew, and by then, Grace was ready to have her mom walk all the way to the bus with her. They did, and Joy stayed by her side till she got on the bus, and it drove off.

Grace still trembled on the way to school. After much convincing thought, she was able to finally believe that school was a safe place, and nobody could get her there. She went on with her school day just fine. At the end of school, as she walked to the buses she remembered her talk with her mom. All she could think about were those fearful words and supposed wicked plans against her. It got her afraid again, and she devised a plan for getting off the bus. The whole ride home, she kept rehearsing these thoughts and plans around in her head. She wasn't going to forget anything. *When I get off at my stop, I'll walk with my neighbor. That way, I'll be close to another person if something is going to happen. When I get in the house, I'll make sure all the doors are locked and the windows closed and blinds shut too. At least now it's light outside. I'll keep my eyes open and watch all around me as I walk home.*

The bus brakes squealed. A loud swoosh of air was released as the driver put out the stop signs and opened the doors. It was already Grace's stop. She did what she was planning to do. Hyperaware of her surroundings, she stayed near the neighbor girl as they walked down the long open dirt road. Even though they walked together, they weren't really together. They weren't friends, but they weren't enemies either. When Grace's home was in view, she relaxed her tensed body and breathed out a sigh of relief. Her mom was there. She breathed in deeply and slowly a few times to settle herself down and slow her heart to a normal pace. She was surely glad her mom was home.

When Grace came through the front doors, homework was not the first order of business. Her mom sat her down and wanted to talk with her about some possible options based on the circumstances. Joy felt something needed to be done to keep her daughter safe. It was obvious to Grace that Joy believed the things Jean told her, which made it hard for Grace not to believe it. She didn't want to believe it, but Fear already took residence in her mind, which controlled her heart.

"I told Hannah about what was going on. She offered to let you stay with them for a while till things get settled and you feel better," Joy presented the first option. Hannah was Grace's older married sister. She was married to Ken Harris a little over a year ago. They lived in that same town but in apartments that were closer to the business streets.

"Or you can choose to go to Oregon with your dad when he comes to take the boys." Joy paused to wait for an answer.

I don't really want to go to Oregon with my dad. He wouldn't take me to church. Moving in with my sister, I'll be safe, and I'll feel peace and get away from this house. I'll still go to the same school. It'll just be easier. It's only for a little bit. For Grace, it was an easy choice. "I'll move in with Hannah."

"Okay, I'll let her know. You can start packing your clothes. You'll stay there tonight."

It was no sooner than when Grace packed all her clothes that Judah walked through the door, back from school himself. Joy informed him and Anthony, who was home the whole time, that Grace was going to be staying at Hannah and Ken's apartment for a while. Judah didn't seem to know what was going on and looked a bit confused. He knew Jean's story. Joy told him earlier that morning before he went off to school but didn't put two and two together. He didn't know Grace was going to move in with Hannah because of what Jean said. He didn't ask any questions. Anthony knew though; he'd been listening to all the hubbub going on.

Just a few minutes passed before they filled up the car with Grace's bags and headed over to the apartment. That evening was spent visiting and talking about the recent happenings. That's when Judah realized why Grace was moving in with Hannah. The words from Jean angered Judah greatly, and he wanted to do something about it. He quietly thought about what he could do to stop anyone from harming his sister. The family talked to Grace again to hear from her own mouth what happened at the trailer about hearing the man's voice talk to Rocky. Everyone seemed to believe Jean's story, which made it harder and harder for Grace to discredit Jean.

Grace didn't want to, or choose to, live in Fear. Since this all seemed to be true, Fear laid his claim on her. After all, Grace was certain some man was talking to her dog, and it was likely that she heard the footsteps, at least once. She fought through thoughts and remembered that she didn't want to believe anything from Jean. *Jean's a witch and probably has psychic abilities. She must have been listening to demons and devils.* It didn't really cross her mind that it was likely that a group of witches and warlocks were behind the planning, and they were the ones going to do it. *So wicked and evil. Maybe Jean knows something. Maybe demons told her what the evil man was planning to do with me—or maybe she's part of the planning. Satan, after all, would know the evil schemes of men, wouldn't he? So Satan could tell Jean what was planned. Yeah, that's how she knows. I thought she was trying to become a Christian.* Grace concluded her thoughts about Jean and thought again, *Maybe this is all true.* Nobody really knew Jean's role in the whole thing except what she told Joy.

Everyone was very supportive of Grace and tried to make her feel as secure as possible. During the discussion, she curled up on the couch as she listened to everyone talk and express how they felt about the whole ordeal. Grace shivered in fear. Hannah noticed and handed her a blanket and told her that she'd be sleeping on that couch, and she could use that blanket. Grace wrapped the blanket around herself and felt warmed, but she was still tensed and visibly shook at the topic at hand.

The rest of the family saw Grace shaken. They changed the subject for her benefit, except for a few last threatening comments from Judah and Ken stating what they would do to this guy if he ever came after Grace. That made Grace feel more confident in her decision to stay at Hannah's. She felt protected. At last, after a few more topics, trying to lighten the mood, Joy, Judah, and Anthony went back home, leaving Grace behind with her caring sister and brother in-law.

Bedtime. Grace stared at the light and shadows coming in through the miniblinds. The apartment's outdoor lighting was on and bright. *If someone walks by, I'll be able to see their shadow.* Time went by, and Grace started feeling drowsy, but she couldn't stop staring and thinking. She turned toward the sofa's backing and covered her head so it was dark, and there was no more light or shadows to think about. She fell asleep.

Chapter 5

Change of Plans

The start of a new week came. They found where the bus was for the apartment complex, and Grace joined one other girl there in the morning. Grace learned her name was Theresa, a thin, gaunt girl, pale-skinned with black coarsely waved hair that went straight across the middle of her back and bangs cut bluntly across the middle of her dark-brown eyes. She wore black lipstick and black clothes. Grace attempted conversations with Theresa any chance she got. Grace got that trait from her mother, Joy.

She had a normal day at school, and it passed by in a flash. When she got off the bus, Theresa was there. Grace was sure to start the conversation and asked her questions. One of the first questions was if she went to church anywhere. Theresa said that she was into witchcraft. Grace usually tried not to judge based from appearances, but based of Theresa's, it wasn't a big shock to her. Grace felt compelled to tell her about Jesus and the way to salvation. There wasn't much response from Theresa, except being a little uncomfortable around the subject. Grace was able to tell the message anyway, as graciously as possible. They parted ways and went into their own apartment. *A witch and into witchcraft? Why are there so many witches around me? Are they trying to spy on me?* Fear taunted her and beat her into a cowering little girl again.

Grace locked the door, kept all the lights off, blinds shut and pointed upward, and lay under the window of the living room. This is the only place she felt comfortable, where nobody could see her if they looked through the window. People watching her, spying on her, planning wicked things against her became her greatest fear, and it controlled her. She was Fear's puppet, and Fear rejoiced at seeing her cower there under the window, motionless on the ground. Fear was successful in paralyzing his victim.

Grace was careful not to breathe too loudly for anyone to hear, not even herself, even though it was ridiculous to think that anyone could actually hear her breathing from outside of the apartment.

She didn't move from that place until she heard the jingling of Hannah's keys, unlocking the door. Grace quickly got up on the couch and sat there, acting like she was just fine before Hannah came in. She was calmed and okay when everyone was awake and in the light with her. That was her safe place: the light and the company of people who loved her.

Bedtime was different. When she was in the room alone with her imagination in the dark, Fear prodded her further into his entanglements. He entangled himself in Grace's mental, emotional, and physical well-being. Fear pushed her further and deeper into isolation as he expanded his territory. Now she wasn't only afraid to be with her mom at home but was also afraid of the night, of the witches around her, and even being at the apartment with Hannah and Ken. The difference was, she was deathly terrified of going back home. Fear was ever present, ever laughing, and ever taunting. He was gaining ground. He was winning.

The next couple days went like this.

It was Tuesday night, everyone in bed, asleep, except Grace. She lay there writhing in fear. It caused her to enter Hannah and Ken's bedroom. She slowly walked to Hannah's side of the bed, wanting to only wake her to tell her that she was afraid, hoping to sleep on the floor in their room instead of the living-room sofa.

"Hannah," Grace whispered. "Hannah." She didn't move, so Grace nudged her a bit. Hannah still didn't wake, so she said in a little bit louder voice, "Hannah, I'm scared."

Ken turned around and saw Grace hovered above Hannah. In reaction, not realizing it was Grace, he yelled out.

Grace ducked down quickly, scared that he might hurt her, not knowing. "It's me, it's me! It's me." Her voice trembled, and she started crying.

"What is going on?" Hannah woke up from the loud yell and commotion.

"She scared me. I saw her standing above you, and I yelled," Ken explained his actions.

"I'm scared," Grace cried quietly, voice quivering, as she stood back up with her blanket wrapped around her.

"Okay, just get in bed. You can lie next to me." Hannah moved over closer to Ken, and Grace was on the edge of the bed. There was hardly any space, but they made it work. It helped Grace sleep for the night. She felt better for the time being. Grace was able to finally get some sleep, and she was grateful that Hannah and Ken were so accommodating.

Wednesday, Joy came by and picked Grace up to go to church. Afterward, when Joy dropped Grace back off at Ken and Hannah's, they went inside to talk. Joy said to Grace, "Grace, I want you to come back home with me."

"Mom, I'm still afraid. I can't come back home."

"Judah and Anthony left this morning with your dad to Oregon. It'll just be me. I want you to come home with me."

"No, Mom, I can't come back, not now, not tonight. Just give me more time. I will come back home with you. I just can't, not right now."

Joy started getting irritated with her daughter and said, "You're coming with me, and that's it."

Hannah and Ken were there. They were getting infuriated with Joy for not listening and trying to force Grace into coming home that night. "Mom, Grace is not going with you. She's scared! Can't you see?"

Joy became frantic and grabbed onto Grace's arms. She started to yank her toward the open door.

"No, I'm not going with you. Mom! I'm staying here!" Grace fought back with all she had. She pulled away, trying to get out of the strong grips of her mother. Grace's eyes burned, her face red, and tears streamed down her face as she fought for what she felt like her life.

If I go with you, I'll die.

"That's it, Mom! Get out of my house now! Let go of Grace!" Hannah yelled out. She intervened with the struggle and was able to loosen her mom's grip on Grace's arms. Grace fell away from Joy as Hannah pushed her mother out the already opened door. "You get out of here and don't come back! You don't do this to Grace! That is not right! You hear me? You don't do this!" She hollered out the door after Joy, who was already walking away.

Grace looked out the door at her mother leaving. Joy looked back at them. Tears filled her eyes, and great sorrow filled her soul as she turned away and walked to her car. Grace felt so bad for her and wanted to go with her, but Fear's grips were stronger than her mother's grips. Grace's hot tears streamed, and she couldn't help but sob.

Grace couldn't believe what was happening. Her family was falling apart in so many ways right before her very eyes. Grace knew Joy just wanted her daughter home with her; she had nobody. Allen abandoned her with divorce. Then Judah and Anthony left with Allen, and now Grace refused to go back home. She would not ever go back knowing there was an evil plan out there to kidnap, rape, and kill her. Joy had nobody else. Grace's heart broke over the whole thing. She knew her mother was hurting, but she just couldn't go home.

Hannah's adrenaline was still high, breathing heavily, eyes flaming and teeth clenched, from the confrontation between her and her mother. Hannah shut and locked the door behind her and asked Grace, "Grace do you want to go to Oregon with Dad?"

Grace couldn't talk yet; she was still choked up with overwhelming emotion, so she just nodded yes, then squeaked out a question, "Didn't Judah and Anthony already leave with him today? Aren't they already gone?"

"Yes, but I'm calling Dad right now." Hannah made an executive decision and closed herself into her bedroom for the phone call.

Grace couldn't hear the conversation.

"Dad, you need to come back and pick up Grace."
"Why? What's happening?"
"She wants to live with and stay with you in Oregon. Last week, Grace came home from school. She was by herself and heard a man talk to Rocky outside. He said, 'Stay there, Rocky.' Rocky didn't bark, and then she heard footsteps outside her bedroom window. It wasn't Judah. He

34

was with Mom and Anthony. Mom told a lady from her church, and the lady told her that someone was planning to kidnap Grace, rape her, and then kill her on the third day. This lady is an actual witch, Dad. Witches do this sort of thing. Grace has been staying with me this week, and she's really scared. Mom tried to get her to come back home and grabbed her, trying to force her to go home with her. Grace was crying and terrified. I think you need to come pick her up to take her with you to Oregon."

"Okay, I'm in Nevada right now. I'm turning around to come get her."

"Thanks, Dad. She's still with me. When will you be here to pick her up?"

"I don't know, probably sometime early in the morning."

"Okay, see you then."

"Okay, bye."

"Bye."

They hung up the phone.

"Grace," Hannah said as she entered the living room, "Dad's going to turn around and come pick you up to live with him. You should make sure all your things are put together."

Grace thought that going with her dad was going to solve her problems, that she wouldn't be afraid when she left the little town in Southern Arizona. *Those people who want to hurt me won't be in Oregon, so I could have peace and safety,* which was all she wanted. Though her eyes were puffy and red from crying, she finally pulled herself together and calmed down. She believed that she was going to beat this nasty plan and beat Fear once and for all when she moved with her dad to Oregon, 1,300 miles away.

Allen, Judah, and Anthony turned around in Nevada. "We're going back."

"Why?" Judah asked.

"Your sister Grace has been going through some stuff, and I'm going to go get her."

"You mean what the witch told Mom? I heard about that. She told Mom that some man was going to kidnap Grace, hide her in a cellar with dirt floors, cedar walls, and cedar steps. That he had an old blue or gray beat-up truck. My friend and I went around the neighborhood looking for the houses with that kind of truck. We knocked on the doors. If it was a nice family or woman with children, we left them alone and said we had the wrong house. If it was a single-looking man, we also told him we had the wrong house but left a death note in his mailbox. We wanted to scare him off if he was the one making those plans."

This next information was eerie and gave Judah goose bumps. He continued, "Dad...we found that cellar. My friends and I were going around the neighborhood and looking for old houses that looked abandoned. We found one when we were snooping around. We saw the cellar, Dad. It was just as the witch described. It a had dirt floor, cedar for walls, and cedar steps too. It was only a few blocks away from Mom's house. I think the plan is real."

There was silence in the car, except the engine and the wheels running their course against the flat straight desert highway. Both of them were quietly convinced that the information given by the witch was plausible, and Grace could be in real danger if left with her mom. Judah didn't sleep for the whole ride, but Anthony was asleep through the whole thing.

It was about two in the morning by the time they turned south off Interstate 10, only fifty minutes away from Hannah's and an hour away from Joy's. The whole time, Judah had been thinking about everything. He thought about his mom, how she would be by herself when Grace left with Dad. He broke the silence, "Dad, I think I should stay with Mom. You know, since Grace will be going with you now."

With that break of silence, Anthony woke up. "What's going on? Where are we?" He recognized where he was; he just wasn't sure why they were there. It appeared they were going back toward Sierra Vista.

"I'm going to go get Grace. She needs to come with me, and Judah is going to stay with your mom now."

"You're going to stay with Mom?" Anthony asked Judah.

"Yeah, I don't think it would be good for her to be by herself. You should stay with Mom too."

"I guess so," Anthony agreed.

"That's a good idea, boys. You take care of your mom and each other."

Judah felt a newfound duty to try to protect his mom, even though he was still a teenage boy and wasn't aware of how that would really look like. He didn't really have a good example from his dad on how to be a man of the house. He just thought living with her and keeping aware would be enough.

"Okay then. I'll call your mother and let her know we're coming by to drop you off first and that I'm picking up Grace to take with me."

Allen took out his cell phone and called Joy. She answered, "Hello."

"Hi. I heard what happened and what's been going on with Grace. I'm on my way to pick her up. She says she wants to go to Oregon with me now. I'm going to drop Judah and Anthony off at your place. They'll stay with you. Then I'll go pick up Grace. I'll be there in about an hour or so."

"Okay…okay. Hannah called earlier and told me Grace was going with you, that you were turning around to come pick her up. I'm glad the boys will stay. That's good." Joy felt defeated from the fight she had at Hannah's apartment but was relieved to know that the boys had decided to stay.

Allen hung up the phone, and Joy held it off the hook as she hunched over and sobbed. "Why, Lord? Why?" she cried out. "Why is this happening to me? This hurts so bad. Please keep my children safe, Lord. Please!" That's all she could say. She hung up the landline, grabbed a blanket, and curled up on the couch. She was going to sit there and wait for her sons to come home. She was glad someone was coming home to her but still upset by all that had happened at Hannah's. She felt dreary, exhausted, and yet quieted. The Lord comforted her, and she began to feel better in her spirit. She understood that somehow everything was going to be okay. God had a plan, even though she herself couldn't understand. From her perspective, nothing made sense, but she was at peace and trusted God and His ways.

Knock, knock, knock—Judah lightly tapped on the door. Joy was a little startled and shook herself awake from drifting off to sleep. She opened the door and let Judah and Anthony in, carrying all their things.

Allen was standing out, away from the door. He wasn't much for words, but considering the circumstances involving both their children, he felt obligated to say something. "I'm sorry this is all happening. I think it's best if I take Grace. If somebody is planning on hurting her, she should go with me."

Joy knew that she agreed, for her daughter's safety at least. "I know… I think it's best too. Be safe."

Allen got in his car and took off. As soon as he pulled away, Joy shut the door and locked it behind her.

Meanwhile at Hannah's, Grace was all packed up, her things by the door. They were all sound asleep, except Hannah. She stayed awake waiting for her Dad's knock. Grace was curled up on the couch with her blanket, exhausted by all the turmoil earlier. The soft knock on the door woke Grace up, but she was expecting it. Hannah heard it too and answered. It was only Allen, and Hannah wondered aloud, "Where's Judah and Anthony?"

"They decided to stay with your mother since Grace is coming with me now. I just dropped them off."

"Oh, okay. That's good." She turned to Grace, who was sleepy-eyed as she pushed herself up from lying down.

"Are you ready to go?" Hannah asked.

"Yeah." She stood up to get her things, but Hannah took hold of her and gave her a big hug.

"I love you, Grace. Everything's going to be okay."

Grace hugged her back. It was awkward; their family rarely hugged. She looked into Grace's eyes, trying to reassure her. Grace looked down and smiled back as she went out the door holding her things. Hannah looked at Allen. "Thanks, Dad. Be safe."

"Yeah. I'll see you later," Allen said.

"Call me when you get there," Hannah made him promise.

"I will." Allen said his goodbyes. He took Grace's things from her, and they walked to the car.

Chapter 6
Fear Follows

What if somebody is watching me go with my dad? They could follow us all the way to Oregon. They can see me now and where I'm at. Fear was gleeful in planting those thoughts in his host, hoping to gain more territory in Grace's heart and mind.

Allen put Grace's things in the trunk of the car. Grace took the back seat so she could lie down and sleep if she wanted to, and he started the long drive to Oregon. Allen had some windows down as he smoked his cigarettes. Grace was left with the sounds of the tires rolling along the road, the air blowing through the windows, and of her thoughts, which nagged at her relentlessly. *They might have seen me go with my dad. The kidnapper has a blue or gray old truck. Who's around? Watch to see if anyone will start to follow us.* Grace looked around her; she didn't see anything in particular that fit any of the descriptions. Plus, nobody was really on the roads that early in the morning in the darkness. Grace was still a bit hyperaware and nervously looking all around every road they passed, making sure they weren't being followed, at the same time trying not to be obvious to her dad. Before they crossed the border checkpoint on Highway 90, she spotted an old truck facing toward them parked on the right side of the road. As they passed it, Grace ducked down into the seat next to her, lying down as far as she could go.

Was that him? Did he hear that I was leaving and he's waiting for me? Did he see me? Does he know I'm in this car and going to follow us? Ugh, this is nonsense. Nobody could know I was leaving town or who'd I be with. I didn't even know until a few hours ago. Grace really tried hard to combat Fear's lies. Fear won again though. Grace lay awake as Fear whispered in her mind, *Make sure nobody can see you. Lie*

43

down and hide. Somebody might see you and follow you. They will find you in Oregon.

Lying there awake, she could see the stars from that angle. It was actually quite beautiful, and she was glad to have something else to think about for a change. It didn't stop her from lying down and checking behind them every so often to make sure they weren't being followed. Eventually, she finally drifted back to sleep.

Allen was the type of person to just drive through and not spend the night anywhere. He kept driving on. Grace woke up when the car suddenly got quiet. It was bright morning. Allen got out of the car and pumped gas at a gas station. Grace ran her fingers through her hair to look presentable. She assumed they'd be going in to use restrooms, get food, and drink too. She was right.

Then they were on the road again and out of that small Nevada town to the straight flat desert highway, where you can see what looks like a mirage from the heat off the pavement, even though it was winter.

Chapter 7

Living with Gramma and Grampa

As they traveled on, Allen revealed that they were going to stay with his mother and stepfather (Grace's grandparents), Gramma and Grampa Moor, as Grace called them, until Allen got a home of his own. Other than that, there was not much to talk about.

Right around midnight, they arrived at Gramma and Grampa Moor's house. It had been two years since Grace had been there last. They were expecting them and had a room ready for Allen to sleep in, and Grace was to sleep on the living-room sofa. It was easy to fall asleep that night, as exhausted as they were from the nonstop drive and it being so late.

Christmas was a week and a half away. Gramma and Grampa Moor had their tree set up and decorated already. Winter Break started that next week for the Central Oregon's public school district. When Allen enrolled Grace in the High Desert Middle School, she wouldn't start until after the public school's winter break would end, which was the Monday after the first weekend in January. This gave

Grace plenty of time to adjust to living there. She didn't have too many problems coping with the move. Moving was something Grace was used to.

What Grace thought would happen after moving to Oregon with her dad was not a reality. To her dismay, Fear followed her all the way to Oregon. Grace was certain those wicked people didn't follow her, so why was she still fearful? She found herself still lying under the windowsill at night on the sofa—quiet, breathlessly frozen, afraid. This continued on until she got a gift on Christmas that started to change her ability to cope and overcome Fear.

Christmas Day came. It was celebrated with Gramma and Grampa Moor at their house, and only Allen's half-brother came to celebrate with them. He was Uncle Jack to Grace. Gramma had everyone sit in the family room early in the morning where the Christmas tree and presents were. Grace was the only child in the room and sat among the three grumpy old men who didn't seem to want to be there. Not at first. Early morning wasn't an agreeable time for the men. But it was Christmas, and they sat there anyway at Gramma's request. Maybe Gramma convinced them to just be there, at least for Grace's sake. Gramma wanted to make it a good Christmas for the only child in the room. After all the trauma Grace had been though, Gramma knew Grace needed something positive. Grace didn't know, but Allen told his mother a little bit of what had gone on in Arizona and why Grace came instead of the boys. Grace didn't know that, though, and Gramma never let on that she knew anything. Gramma was the most cheery in the room and made things the least awkward as possible as she ran the show. Eventually the three—Grampa, Allen, and Uncle Jack—relaxed and started to enjoy being a part of a family Christmas.

"Grace, can you hand these to your dad?" Gramma asked.

Without a word, Grace nodded and got right up to hand out the gifts as Gramma sorted through them.

"These are for Uncle Jack." Grace handed the next bundle to her uncle. Gramma gathered the next bundle together for Grampa. "These are for Grampa." Grace leaned over to grab them, still standing in the middle of the room, and handed them to Grampa.

Gramma had another pile left on the floor next to herself. She handed Grace one box. "Grace, I want you to open this one first." Gramma Moor handed Grace a small box about the width of both of her hands, heavy for its size. "Go ahead, open it."

Grace looked at her for a second, making sure she followed instruction and wondering, *Is this it? It doesn't matter, just sit down. Where?* Grace looked around the room and sat on the sofa opposite of the tree, away from everyone else. She started to open it slowly, trying not to rip the paper.

"You can rip it open. Go ahead, just tear it up!" Gramma gently encouraged.

Uncle Jack broke the ice. He had the best sense of humor of them all. He laughed as he said quite loudly, "Oh, come on! Just rip the paper open! Rip it! Rip it open. What are you trying to do? Open it daintily? Trying not to rip it so you could use it later? What are you going to use

that paper for? Just rip the darn thing." He laughed, and then everyone else laughed.

Grace's cheeks grew rosy. She was embarrassed but realized how silly she must have looked. It helped Grace lighten up and just go at it. It was Christmas after all. Grace was a kid and should be as any kid on Christmas Day— happy. All eyes were watching, but Grace didn't want to hold everyone up. Apparently, they were all waiting on her. She tore open the paper and found a large pack of AA batteries. She looked up at her gramma, lifted it up for everyone to see, and smiled with slight confusion. *Is this a joke?* Everyone chuckled.

"Okay, Grace, here's your next present." Gramma reached out to hand her another box.

I knew that wasn't my only present. Grace got up and took her seat a little closer to her gramma at the tree, a little less rigid.

"Go ahead, open it now! We want to see what Santa got you." Gramma smiled a warm smile, looking forward to seeing Grace's reaction to this next gift.

Santa? Grace laughed under her breath about the idea that Gramma though she believed in Santa. *It's probably something I can use the batteries with. I have no clue what, though.* Grace didn't know what to expect next. This time, she tore the wrapping paper off, not about to be teased by Uncle Jack again. It was a portable compact disc (CD) player that came with headphones. Everyone *ooh*ed and *aww*ed, and Grace was delighted to have her own CD player. It was something that many kids had. Now she had one with enough batteries to last a lifetime, she thought. There was one problem: she wouldn't be able to use it as she had no

CDs of her own. Allen's gift to Grace was money so that she could pick out her own gift later that week. Gramma suggested, "Maybe you can get some CDs that you like now." Grace liked that suggestion and liked shopping for her own things.

Gramma and Grampa also got Grace a few more presents, some clothes, as she was going to start a new school after winter break and wanted her to feel confident in herself. Everyone opened their gifts, but Grace paid no attention. She was trying to get the CD player out of its hard plastic packaging.

When everyone was done, Uncle Jack came out with a stack of about twelve CDs. "Here, Grace. Look through these. If you see something you like, keep it. This is my gift to you." They were from his personal CD collection. There was quite a range of music. Grace recognized only a couple artists, though they were all secular. She wasn't really familiar with most music, unless it was Christian. Even then, she only knew what the Christian radio played. That's all Grace and Joy listened to in Arizona. That day, Grace spent going through and listening to the CDs that Uncle Jack brought out, trying to determine if she liked any of them. Most of them, she did not like and didn't need to listen to more than one song. She ended up picking out three—Fiona Apple, Selena, and Mariah Carey—and gave the rest back to Uncle Jack. She liked the soft, even, soothing sounds of some of the songs. *Maybe this can help me sleep at night. Some of these songs are so pretty. I can listen to them and fall asleep. What good gifts.*

Out of the three CDs Grace took, she tried listening to Fiona Apple to figure her music out, whether or not she really liked it. Grace started becoming more concerned about the lyrics. They just didn't seem to settle with her and made her feel uneasy or off. It took her a few days to decide that she wasn't going to listen to Fiona Apple anymore and gave that CD back. Grace began to feel a deep innate conviction in her soul to not listen to things that were promoting blatant sin. She favored the other two CDs more and only a few songs from each. They seemed pretty harmless and neutral, and she enjoyed their beautiful voices. Even though she tried to believe that the songs were neutral, she still couldn't convince herself that they actually were. Something was telling her inside that anything that was without God was still godless. Inside, Grace was left unsatisfied.

The next few nights, Grace experimented with seeing if she could lull Fear with the music so she could sleep better. It did, in fact, lull Fear. Grace was able to physically sleep but felt emptied, unsatisfied, and unrested. It just wasn't enough. Grace had been grasping at the wind of sorts to get what she's been looking for and needing. All Grace found was that whatever it was that she was trying to catch—soul peace wasn't actually there at all. It was all an empty promise. A lie—Deception.

Fear and Deception took turns and tried to trick her, making her think that what she was doing was working. Grace was unaware, but they were playing tag team. They rejoiced that Grace seemed to be buying it. That was as far as they could tell. The only way Grace could describe the feeling was that it was similar to what she felt when she was at Jean's house. Something still was not right. Though Fear was quelled when the music played, the fact that the music had no God didn't solve anything for her. These attempts were like a Band-Aid of sorts to cover up spiritual trauma, wounds, and sickness. She didn't like what she was feeling but still didn't have the answer—with exception of a pull toward, *Only God has the cure.* Grace knew these feelings were spiritual, and she needed something spiritually good with God in it to make her feel better. In so doing, she came up with her own conclusion: find things with God in it.

The next weekend came, and Allen didn't have to work.

"Dad, can we go shopping? I want to buy something with the money you gave me for Christmas."

"Yeah, we can go shopping. Where do you wanna go?"

"I want to buy a new CD, so anywhere they sell CDs, I guess."

Allen took Grace to a supermart in town, one of the big-box stores that has almost everything. Since Grace knew what she wanted and Allen was an in-and-out kind of person, they went straight to the isles that sold CDs. Grace quickly found the Christian section. She wasn't familiar with specific artists; all she really listened to before she had the CD player of her own was the radio. She found a disc that had multiple artists. It was the year's top 30 Christian artists and songs. She recognized a lot of the songs and found what she wanted. It was the biggest bang for her buck.

Every night after that, at Gramma and Grampa's, Grace fell asleep only to the Christian music. She still liked the other music, but she felt much better about listening to music that had God in it.

Every so often, Fear crept up on her, especially when nobody else was at home or at night. So Grace turned to the Christian music and felt better. She listened to the God-glorifying lyrics, and that seemed to shut Fear up for the time being. The songs she listened to contradicted, counteracted, combatted Fear's lies. She started to feel a hope and saw a dim light at the end of a long dark tunnel. Her hope came from the glimpse of light shown to her through Christian music. She now knew which direction to head, and that was to God Himself. He is that light.

Chapter 8

Allen and Grace Move Out

Before Grace had to attend school, Allen found a place to move into. Allen took Grace to look at it, and Grace's first impression was *yuck*. Grace didn't really have a say; Allen had already signed a realtor contract and was going to close within the month. Allen was a handyman and had plans to renovate the place to make it more livable, but they still had to move in as it was. The lot was on an unkept half an acre, twice as long as it was wide. The double-wide trailer had paneling on the outside, and when you walked in, there was a living room to the right, which had inside/outside carpeting, a window facing the front of the home and one facing the back, with dirty old stained miniblinds, some bent up. To the left was the dining and kitchen areas with linoleum floors. The dining area had an old broken-down built-in hutch that was falling apart and was either missing shelves or the shelves were hanging down, broken. The kitchen's cupboards and drawers were well worn and dirty, and it had older appliances.

Down the hall to the left was one of the two bedrooms. It was the one Grace was going to stay in. The door was missing; the miniblinds were broken up and hanging off the strings too. The opposite side of the hall was the bathroom and a mudroom with laundry hookups and the door to the backyard. At the end of the hall was the master bedroom that had a master bathroom. Grace was not excited to move into this old broken-down trailer, but Allen worked hard to make it suitable enough to live in.

Grace started going to High Desert Middle School, and when she was gone, Allen spent much time and effort in the house. He tore out the old hutch, got Grace a new door and painted it in the color of Grace's choice, and installed new miniblinds to replace all the dirty old broken ones. Allen purchased a new twin-sized bed and allowed

Grace to pick out her own sheets and comforter. Allen acquired an old hide-a-bed sofa from a yard sale. Among the first things he got was a flat-screen TV, a TV stand, and started up a satellite TV service. He cleaned out the kitchen and got household groceries and items. Some were given to him by Gramma and Grampa Moor. The trailer became more livable and comfortable enough to sustain them. Allen made do with what he had and did a great job.

At High Desert Middle School, Grace had a hard time catching up with whatever the students were learning in her classes, especially science and history. She was put in the middle of whatever they had been working on prior (it wasn't the same as what she was learning in Arizona). For one of Grace's school projects, she was to create a floor-plan and use foam core for the walls and floors and leave the top open and exposed for viewing. She decided to redesign the trailer they now lived in. She altered the floor-plan a little bit and made updates. Later on, Allen actually used her new updated floor-plan school project to make renovations on the trailer, just as she designed it. But that wasn't completed for years down the road and was done a little at a time. As far as making new friends, she never really felt like she was accepted or belonged to any group. Though, she did hang out with a few students who tolerated her. Such was the remainder of her seventh-grade year in school.

Homelife was a different story for her. That's where she learned about life and spiritual things. The things that seemed to matter more than nominal public school, the basics of school subjects, and just being part of the herd.

Growth in life and spirituality happened at home, although home didn't have much when it came to activities. The daily routine of waking, going to school, coming to an empty home, spending time alone until Allen came home from wherever, and then sleep again left Grace with a lot of time to think and come up with her own understanding of the world around her. No person was there to instruct her in it, just the invisible hand of God. God led her mind, soul, spirit, and body toward His light. When she got a glimpse of His light the first time, it was truly irresistible. She also found that Fear hid from the light of God. So even with that aspect, the light became even more compelling, and she so desired to dwell in it. She began to search God out.

Grace was taken away from the environment that caused her to meet Fear to begin with. Since then, Fear never left her side, except for when she was in light. Until then, Fear had been a dreaded companion, waiting for her each day at any opportune time. She was usually home alone; sometimes she had only a few minutes of solitude, sometimes hours until late night. Through trial and error, Grace was learning that the opposite of Fear was God. At the time, she relied heavily on content that she believed to contain God, not knowing how to reach Him any other way. Not knowing that God wasn't One to be contained by content. She just didn't know any better. She had her Christian music, she had a Bible, and she had television shows that were Christian-based. She did not have church or anybody Christian in Oregon to mentor her.

The times Grace was home alone was when she had to make her choices. She knew she couldn't stand or be sustained in Fear's company, so she immediately went to something that would drown out those incessant whisperings. As a twelve-year-old, she naturally turned to the easiest and most convenient option: television. It was her number one choice. She really despised reading; she found it very difficult to read at all. She fought with dyslexic tendencies and many times would have to read things over and over again just to understand what she was reading. She left the music to falling asleep so she could close her eyes and drift off. This was the answer for her for now.

It wasn't until one day she heard a message on the television about fear that she was finally able to understand and have answers for the real solution—answers that were going to dispel Fear for good and change her life forever.

Grace came home from school one day. She didn't have homework to do, so she just made herself a sandwich and sat to watch TV. She was home alone and wasn't sure when her dad would be back, so she went through her normal routine and turned to the Christian channel. Much of what she watched didn't appeal to her. Some of it seemed elementary, old fashioned, fake, or she just didn't agree with it based on what she had learned in the past. *It's better than nothing and better than Fear.* Then in one of the teachings, something piqued her interest.

"Do you have fear in your life?"

Yes, I do. I need to watch this. What is he going to say? Maybe this is the answer to getting rid of my Fear problem. Grace perked up and postured herself to hear every bit of what was to be said next. She turned up the volume to ensure nothing would be missed and even rushed out to grab a pencil and her journal to take notes.

"If you have fear, it's because you don't know God."

What do you mean "I don't know God"? I believe in Jesus to be my Savior. I believe He died on the cross for my sins. I believe all the Bible stories. I believe God and in Him.

"There are three things you need in order to know God," the preacher continued to explain. The first thing he spoke of was the Gospel, the salvation message of Jesus, and being born again in the Spirit—putting your complete belief and trust in Jesus to save you and to guide you in life and all things pertaining to life.

Yes, yes, I believe in these things. One down, two to go. What else do I have to do to "know God" so that Fear will leave me alone? Grace jotted down as much as she could in her journal.

"The next thing you need to do is to pray. What is prayer? Praying is talking to God, speaking with Him, and spending time with Him. When you are saved, you should try and get to know God. To know anybody you meet, you have to spend time with them, right? Same with God. You need to spend time with God, talking with Him, and getting to know Him."

Grace was busy taking in all the information, and as she took her notes, the knowledge of a relationship with God started to sink in. *So it's not just about knowing about God. It's about knowing Him. Okay. What's the last thing?*

"The last thing you need to do is read your Bible! How do you know who God is unless you read about who He is? One way to know what is true about God and what is not. The Bible contains the character of God, who He is in essence. The Bible contains all truth about God. If you know God and you are saved, then you will know that you don't have to have fear. Fear will have to flee. You see, fear is associated with punishment. If you are saved, you will not have to face the eternal punishment of hell. You are eternally secure and will be in His peace. First John chapter 4, verse 18 says, 'There is no fear in love, but perfect love casts out fear. For fear has to do with punishment, and whoever fears has not been perfected in love.' God is love, folks. If you know God and become perfected in His love, then that love will cast out all fear. You need to not only know about God, you need to know Him."

The program was concluded, and a commercial turned on. Grace thought she better start right away and turned off the television so she could focus.

That's it? I can do that! One, have faith and believe in Christ to be my Savior. I do already. Done. Two… Grace looked down at her notes. *Pray. Wow, I never really thought about talking to God.* Grace knew Christians prayed, but the purpose of prayer was never clear to her until now. *I thought I knew the Bible stories, and that was good enough. It's not about knowing about God but knowing God,* she reminded herself. *So praying to talk to God, to know Him.* She eyed her notes to make sure that was how it was said. *Pray. I better start.* Grace didn't waste any time. She got on her knees and bowed low on the ground and started to pray. "Dear God, I do believe in Your Son Jesus. I do believe He is my Savior, that He died on the cross to save me from my sins. Lord, You know that I have Fear, and it's been with me and following me. You know all things. I ask in the name of Jesus that this Fear would be taken away from me. I pray that I will be perfected in Your love and that it would cast out all this Fear in my life. I don't want it anymore. I want to be done with it. I want peace, Lord. I ask this in Jesus's name. Please cover this household with Your angels. Guard it and my heart so that I will have Your protection and

truth in my heart, knowing all about You. Help me do these things. Help me read the Bible, and understand who You are even more. I ask this in Jesus's name, amen."

Grace felt more confident as her faith in God was established. The light of God enveloped her, and she really truly became free in that moment. But she wasn't done. *Now what? Third thing.* Again referring to her notes, she read, *Read the Bible. I know I have my Bible somewhere.* Grace brought a Bible with her from Arizona. She never opened it but knew she wanted to keep it with her. She knew it contained those stories and God's truth, but again she hated to read. This time, she was determined to read it no matter what and no matter how hard it was. She was desperate to get rid of Fear once and for all. She needed sure deliverance, and she needed it now. She was tired and wearied from all the damage Fear did on her heart, mind, and soul. She suddenly felt strengthened from the prayers and asked herself where she should start. *Revelation. This tells the future.*

Grace had gotten her interest of the future from her mother, Joy, but she knew she wanted God telling her the future, not some witch speaking on behalf of the devil. *This witch tried telling me what my future was, but I need to know God's future.* That was it, her deciding factor. She found her Bible and lay on the ground where she had prayed. She opened the Bible to Revelation and started to read it. Churches, pillars, stars, dragons, angels, lamp stands, beasts, scrolls, bowls, seals, lion, lamb, saints, multitudes, numbers, battles, the end of the world, and heaven. Grace comprehended barely anything she was reading. The thing she understood the most was the promises at the end of the book. This was of great comfort, even though she didn't really understand the other things she read.

Toward the end of the book, Grace's dad, Allen, walked through the door. He saw her on the ground reading the Bible. He was a bit shocked; this wasn't usually something that Grace was found doing when he got home. Usually, she was watching television, doing homework, eating, or cleaning. Allen chose to settle in the house the way he usually did. He went into his room for a bit and then came back out and got something to eat. Grace remembered her dad telling her that he had read the whole Bible before, or she thought she heard that at some point. When Grace's dad came back out and walked past her, she said, "Hey, Dad. I'm reading Revelation. I don't really understand what it means. Can you tell me what it means?"

"Well, you have to read the whole Bible to understand it."

The whole Bible? That's a lot. It's impossible for me. Reading is too hard. Well, he doesn't want to talk about the Bible. I know he's not really following God right now anyway. Grace let completing the task of reading the Bible for the day be good enough, even if she didn't understand most of it. She felt good, better than she'd felt in a long time. These were her first steps in faith. She wasn't about to let the lessons of "knowing God" get away from her. she clung to it and engaged in praying every day thereafter. Reading, however, proved to be a more difficult task. She didn't do it every day—if anything, a chapter or a few verses here and there when she remembered or felt motivated.

Chapter 9
Grace's New Relationship

This new relationship made Grace a new creation in heart, mind, and soul. She began to feel a deep connection with the Divine, with God Himself, the Great I AM. He personalized His covenant relationship with Grace. She recognized who God was to and for her. God revealed Himself to Grace by being the God that He is for eternity's past, present, and future.

Grace was introduced to God not by His names, per se, but by what some of those names represented.

Jehovah-Nissi

> She was no longer vexed.
> She no longer felt the need to cower at the
>   suggestions of Fear.
> Anytime Fear tried to peak his ugly head
>   into Grace's mind, she would pray,
>   and Fear would have to go.
> God was, is, and ever will be the
>   conqueror and victor over spirits

whose purpose is to steal, kill, and
destroy.
Grace's Jehovah-Nissi.

El Elyon

God was, is, and ever will be eternal,
mighty, strong, and powerful on
Grace's behalf.
Grace's El Elyon.

Adonai

Grace made God her Master, her Lord.
She'd given herself completely to God
for Him to command.
She was under His ultimate protection.
God was, is, and ever will be her Adonai.

Jehovah

God revealed Himself to Grace and showed
her grace.
God dwelled with her as she was His child
now who was mysteriously born of the
Spirit.
And through the Holy Spirit, He guided and
delivered her.
Grace found herself praising and
worshipping God in spirit and truth
more and more every day.
He was, and is, and always will be
Grace's Jehovah.

Jehovah-Shalom

God satisfied and filled Grace's deepest
    needs in her human heart.
He gave her peace that did not depend on
    any circumstance that Grace found
    herself in, eternally without
    beginning or end,
Grace's Jehovah-Shalom.

Jehovah-Rophe

God restored everything that spiritual
    enemy stole from Grace.
He cured her mentally, physically, and
    spiritually and sustained her.
God, Grace's faithful Jehovah-Rophe.

El Shaddai

God was, is, and always will be all-
    sufficient, satisfying and nourishing.
God blessed Grace abundantly, not with
    material means but was blessed with
    every spiritual blessing.
Grace's ever satisfying El Shaddai.

Jehovah-Rohi

What love, what intimacy, what concern,
    what tender care, provision, and
    guidance Grace received from God.

Not momentarily, but from the days
    she was led to seek God, to the day
    she met with God, and put her whole
    trust in Jesus as her Savior, and will
    be to the end of her life on earth and
    beyond,
Grace's Jehovah-Rohi.

Jehovah-Shammah

God was ever present.
He promised never to leave His children
    nor forsake them.
The promise keeper to stay present, to
    provide security and protection with
    everlasting fellowship with Himself,
    through His Holy Spirit on earth and
    until the day He gathers His chosen to
    meet with them face-to-face for the
    rest of eternity.
Grace's Jehovah-Shammah.

Grace didn't know these names at the time, but she experienced the depths of the meanings of these names of God. These precious truths she possessed as treasures. Riches that no thief, man, or spirit could steal. They were hers forever.

Each day that passed, Grace felt freer, stronger, and more confident in God and His power over the demonic activities that at their feeble attempts tried to ensnare her again and again. Fear and Deception that once gripped and controlled Grace had become Fear's own fatal attempts, like an enemy falling into his own traps and devices. Fear's visitations were less often and became shorter and shorter as Grace learned to wield her newfound weapons: weapon of the truth of God and prayer against demonic spirits.

The unction and power of the Holy Spirit in her life was evidence of God Himself. He won every spiritual battle Grace faced. There were no doubts that this was a real and true relationship and not fables. This was not just the stories that Grace believed. She still believed those stories, but now she knew the God of those stories, of history—His story. Grace could not deny what she has witnessed of God in her own life. Not only of His salvation, His deliverance, and His spiritual blessings but much more.

Out of habit, Grace would listen to the Christian music at nights to fall asleep. Sometimes she would forget to pray and just turn to the music for comfort. Sometimes she would pray and then turn it on. Other times, she would turn it on, remember to pray, pray, and then turn it on again. This all to say that Grace still relied pretty heavily on Christian music for sleep and rest at night.

One night after Grace prayed, she turned on the music. Halfway through the first song, she felt the urge to turn it off. The Spirit spoke to her heart. She did not hear an audible voice, but the message could not have been clearer:

> *Grace, I have shown you my power over Fear.*
> *You are relying on music to give you peace*
>   *and sleep.*
> *Now rely on Me to give you peace and rest.*
> *It is not the music you need; it is Me.*
> *Turn off the music and rely on Me.*

Wow, this is true. God, You delivered me from Fear, and here I am, relying on music to get me to sleep, but here You are. You, Yourself. Please forgive me for using music to replace You. You are my peace, my rest. I rest in You, Grace prayed in her thoughts. The warmth of God's Spirit filled her chest and her whole being, soul, spirit, as well as her body. *Is this what it means to be in the arms of Christ?* It was like she was a little girl again, sitting under the warmth and protection of her father, but this time, her Heavenly Father. This was, in fact, what she was searching for all along. She finally grasped the light, and it was tangible through God. She had soul peace. She was at rest with nothing but her and God, and that astounded her. She was truly in awe and admiration of her Lord. This was the beginning of Grace allowing God to be her all in all. God became her everything, her peace, and her source. She didn't need the things of this world; all she needed was God. She knew that from then on that nothing else could satisfy her, and nobody else could sustain her. What a precious moment she spent with God. It impacted her trust in God for the rest of her life. God dwelt with Grace and Grace with God in the warmth of His loving arms.

Being human, Grace was far from perfect and made many mistakes before and after her own relationship with God. These trespasses were both known and unknown to her. God—eternally holy, perfect, and just—was rich in mercy (compassionate and forgiving when her sin deserved to be punished) and grace (receiving God's favor, even though she didn't deserve it). This caused Grace to want to do and be better out of love, admiration, and appreciation for God's surpassing forgiveness.

She loved this good God, but He loved her better and loved her first. Even while she was still a sinner, even before she knew Him, He knew her. He knew Grace was living in transgression against His divine laws. He knows all things (an attribute of his divine nature—omniscience); this is so for all mankind. The plan of old from the beginning of time, God ordained, He prophesied, and in His sovereignty, made it come to pass, the provision of redemption for mankind. Redemption for His chosen, His elect, His children that would ever be born of the Spirit. God sent His Son, Jesus, to earth to pay for Grace's transgressions by death on the cross, though innocent and sinless Himself, so that at the right time, Grace could believe in Him and be saved. What grace! What forgiveness! By grace through faith, her sins were paid for by the acts of Jesus. Not only did He die for her transgression, He conquered sin and death by rising back to life again three days later. He took the keys of Hades and is now able to set the prisoners of sin and death free into eternal life for those who will believe and put their faith in Jesus and His work. The blackness of sin that marked and stained Grace's life was wiped clean by the blood sacrifice of Jesus. The payments of her sin was death, but Jesus paid it all.

On God's side of the relationship, at the moment of Grace's faith, she became justified, declared righteous in His sight. She was declared holy as God is Jehovah-N'kaddesh, One who makes you holy. This wasn't because Grace was ever good enough; it was God's love and unmerited favor to take the punishments upon Himself. For it was by God's grace that Grace was set free from her own sin and the second death of hell. God bestowed upon His new child,

Grace, born of the Spirit, not only salvation but grace, mercy, justification, sanctification (the work God does in the life of the Christian to become more holy in their journey), and protection from the one who comes to steal, kill, and destroy. There are infinite virtues and attributes to God; some will eventually be revealed and made known to Grace. She will never understand God fully, but the things He reveals, she will know and be eternally blessed by them.

So it was not by Grace's ability to keep ahold of her own salvation, because she is not capable, but wholly dependent on God's ability to keep all that are His. He has not lost one and will never lose any. "For I am sure that neither death nor life, nor angels nor rulers, nor things present nor things to come, nor powers, nor height, nor depth, nor anything else in all creation, will be able to separate us from the love of God in Christ Jesus our Lord" (Romans 8:38–39). These truths became Grace's incorruptible treasures. She was very rich indeed.

Chapter 10

Mental Preparation

It was now the start of the second week in June, and her seventh grade school year was nearing the end. Grace turned thirteen in February. Her relationship with God was only a few months old, and her spiritual battles became easier and easier to deal with. She remained uninvolved with social activities, church, or anything outside of school and home routines and an occasional visit with Gramma and Grampa Moor. These were all the opportunities Grace had while living with Allen, but she didn't mind the slow pace. It was then that she finally was awakened and regenerated in spirit in order that she would see, know, and hear God calling her unto salvation, to be born again in spirit, and to be saved. That calling was irresistible, and she answered it.

In a couple days, Grace would go back to Arizona to live with her mom, Joy. As she thought about it, she wondered how she would react going back home to her mother's house. *Was someone going to be waiting for me to carry out that awful plan when I get back to Arizona? It's been six months. They probably gave up. So probably not. Certainly the people involved didn't follow me here. I know that for a fact. Fear followed me, though. I couldn't run away from Fear. With God, I faced Fear, and God delivered me from it. I know now that God is with me no matter where I am. He's helped me get rid of being afraid. He's helped me overcome and be at peace. I can go back to Arizona and be at peace too. Fear followed me to Oregon, but now that I have God. He will always be with me wherever I go. I will continue what I've learned here, and God will be my protection, my help, my peace, just like He is here.* In Oregon, Fear for life was diminished down to nothing. Fear and Deception tried to collaborate and came up with a new purpose and tactic against Grace and became Fear of the Unknown, but it didn't work. Grace knew God would be with her whether here, there, or anywhere. Grace was triumphant in Oregon, and she was determined to be triumphant in Arizona too.

Grace excitedly thought about going to church again. This time, she had a real relationship with God Himself. The thought of being a part of His church brought much anticipation. Being able to learn and grow in spiritual matters and have the Bible taught to her gave her confidence that she would find success in the unknown future. This also dispelled Fear calling out the unknowns and the what-ifs. She didn't read much of the Bible in Oregon herself; the big book overwhelmed her. So sitting in on Bible teaching was something she craved the most. It was a hunger that she's never had before, a hunger not in body but in soul and spirit. She was excited knowing that God has a real purpose for her and that she could start functioning in whatever role God put her in. A role she didn't feel there was an opportunity to fulfill with her dad. Church had a whole new meaning and purpose for Grace's life. As Grace prepared for her return to Arizona, she was granted strength by remembrance. She remembered God's faithfulness and where He's brought her from. She remembered how powerfully He had acted on her behalf in such a short time, when she was the only Christian around, when it was just her and God.

Chapter 11
Living with Joy

It was time. Grace packed up all her clothing, preparing for that long trip her dad only like to take a day on. With all her clothes packed, Grace set her alarm to wake her up at midnight, and they both went to bed by 8:00 p.m. Allen was planning to leave early enough so they could drive through and make it that same day.

The drive was uneventful. Grace took the early part of the drive to sleep. She slept most of the morning, except when Allen stopped to get gas, food, and to use the restroom.

They drove on, until they finally arrived at Ken and Hannah's apartment really late and spent the rest of the night there.

At around eight o'clock the next morning, Joy showed up with Judah and Anthony. Joy sported a big smile as she went to hug Grace. It was a long time spent without her daughter, and she missed her dearly. Grace smiled and gave her a hug back. Though they weren't really a hugging kind of family, she tolerated it.

The last time Joy saw Grace was at Hannah's. Last time, it was awful a situation of being yelled at and kicked out by Hannah, along with Grace, filled with tears, fear, and trembling, refusing to go back home. For both of them, it was a raw memory. What a different kind of situation they found themselves in that morning. Much more peace, control, and even joy over the reunion of the children with their parents and siblings. Although there was a bit of awkwardness because Allen was there too. He didn't like being around Joy now that the divorce was final; he didn't want to give Joy any ideas of possible reconciliation and remained quiet, unless it was business.

A discussion started as Hannah gathered the adults around the kitchen table and started questioning for information and helped create parenting plan for Joy and Allen. Hannah felt as if she had to be the mediator between her parents and spurred on the conversation to figure it out. "Hey, Grace, do you plan on staying with Mom for the school year or Dad?"

"I would like to be with Mom during the school years and Dad over the summers from now on," Grace answered from the couch.

Grace was joined by Judah and Anthony. All Judah said was, "Hi."

Grace said hi back.

Anthony looked over at her from the ground and said hi too.

"Hi, Anthony!" She said with a smile. They shook hands as a joke because they didn't ever hug. When it came to sentiment, all of them took after Allen. It seemed that just being in the same room was good-enough company. They sat together with the television on, and Grace eavesdropped on the conversation of the adults. The whole family at Hannah's apartment was together, but still very much broken apart.

"Judah, what do you want to do?" Hannah continued.

"I want to be with Dad for school and Mom for summers," Judah answered. That didn't surprise Grace; she expected that answer. That was what they originally wanted before that whole ordeal Fear created through the witch's so-called telling of the future. She also expected that answer from Anthony, who answered the same question next.

"You Anthony?"

"Same as Judah," Anthony answered shortly.

It seemed fair enough; each parent would have at least one child with them year round. That way, neither parent would be left alone. Though Grace didn't have much of a relationship with her brothers Judah and Anthony, she was secretly bummed that she wouldn't be near them. She enjoyed their company, even if it was quiet company. Being away made her heart grow fonder of her family.

Grace tried listening to the conversation as it continued on, though it was quieter since it was only with those around the table, and the TV was on.

"Dad, do you want to come back and pick up Judah and Anthony when school starts in Oregon in September?"

"No, I don't really want to make a whole other trip. I don't have money for that. Why don't I just take the boys now, and then after the next school year, I'll bring them back when I pick up Grace for the summer," Allen answered plainly. It seemed fair enough for everyone. Money wasn't something that either parent had much of, so it only made sense to make it work that way, with the least amount of traveling.

Joy was in agreement and said, "That's fine. I understand. I'll have to take the boys back home to get their things though."

"Dad, you're welcome to stay here for another night or two, get some rest, and allow Judah and Grace some time together, as well as letting them pack their things. If you want," Hannah offered.

"Maybe one more night. I'll just take a nap this afternoon and sleep tonight. I can make it back just fine. The boys can get their things today, and then we'll leave tomorrow early morning." Allen was firm in his decision.

"That's fine, whatever you want to do Dad," Hannah complied.

"Well, I guess I can take the kids back home with me and let the boys pack up their stuff. I'll bring them back later this evening after dinner," Joy stated her part of the plan.

So it was, everything was planned out; there wasn't much more to say. Each knew what they had to do, and it wasn't long before Joy called to the kids to get going. "Hey, we're going to go home. Your dad wants to leave tomorrow so you boys will have to pack your things. I'll bring you back here when we're done after dinner," Joy explained to the kids. Grace got her bags, and they all left. Joy seemed a bit upset but tried not to show any emotion. Saying goodbye to any of her children was never an easy thing to do; neither was knowing that Grace and the boys won't really get much time spent together. Joy made sure they took their time. She wanted to make the most out of the time given to them to be together before they were separated again.

When they got home to the single-wide trailer, Rocky, the family pet, greeted Grace excitedly. He remembered her

and wagged his curled tail with great enthusiasm. Rocky bowed low with his front legs, leaving his wagging tail up in the air. Grace was happy to see him too; she brought him inside and forgot about her bags. The boys wasted no time packing their things; they basically threw their clothes into backpacks and were done in less than half an hour. Grace and Joy sat in the living room. Joy had lots of questions about Grace's time in Oregon since they didn't talk over the phone. When Judah and Anthony were done, they put their bags at the door and joined them.

The witch's prediction last December became the topic of discussion. Joy really wanted to know that her daughter was going to be okay staying home with her. Judah, not of many words, finally spoke about what he did around the neighborhood, revealing too that he and his buddy did see that cellar described as Jean said it would be. It was the same story he told Allen on their way back to get Grace from Hannah's. Neither Joy nor Grace knew any of that; it was news to them both. Grace felt admiration inside knowing that her brother actually stood up for her and acted on her behalf to protect her. She felt like this created a bond and connection with her brother that she never had before. She didn't think that what he did was necessarily godly, but it showed her that he cared about her. This was Judah's way of trying to show Grace he did, in fact, care, even though they wouldn't be together over the next few years with exception of two, summer and school, yearly exchanges. This brought Joy to wonder, so she asked, "How have you been doing with all of that stuff?"

"I've been doing better. I started praying, and God really helped take away the fear."

"Do you still have fear?"

"No, I don't feel afraid anymore. I know God is with me and that He's protecting me."

Joy tilted her head in an awed expression and mouthed the word, "Wow!" and then said out loud, "God is with you, Grace. I'm very proud of you for seeking God. He does protect you, and I'm glad you know that too!" Joy got up and walked to the bathroom, leaving Judah, Anthony, and Grace to talk and visit. When she got in there, she closed the door. Hot tears streamed down her face and sat on the side of the tub and quietly prayed with heartfelt thanksgiving. "Thank You, God! You've brought my daughter back to me. I know you don't waste anything. *All* bad situations, You've been able to turn around for Your glory and our good. Praise You, Jesus. Thank You, God, for delivering Grace from all her fears. You amaze me! You are so good!" She sat there, her head lifted up as she felt the heavy, comforting, warm hand of God touching her heart. She sat in awe, rejoicing, and smiled up as she dried her tears. God turned her sorrows into joy, her mourning into gladness. She sat, calmed and radiant, for a few moments longer. She finally came back out, more composed, but Grace could tell that she had been crying. *It's probably because the boys will be leaving after dinner*, Grace thought. They spent the rest of the afternoon catching up.

"I better start dinner. We'll eat dinner together, and then I'll take you back to Hannah's, okay?" Joy informed the boys when evening approached.

"Okay," Judah answered.

Joy started dinner, and when she was waiting for it to cook, she asked Grace, "Hey, did you bring in your bags?"

"No, I'll get them now." She went out and got her bags from the back seat of the car and brought them in.

"Hey, Grace," Joy continued. "I'm going to let you choose which bedroom you want to sleep in, wherever you feel more comfortable, okay? And I'll sleep in the other room."

Grace didn't think about that. The room she was in, before when the whole ordeal began, the windows were larger and closer to the center of the walls, closer to where her bed would be. The other bedroom had two smaller widows near the ceiling, and the bed would be farther away from the windows. *Yeah, pick the one with the smaller, higher windows. It would be harder to see through them.* Fear started speaking to her. Grace recognized his voice. *Yep, Fear followed me all the way back here. I don't have to be afraid, but it would probably feel more comfortable in that room.* "I think I want to stay in the room by the bathroom." That was the one with the smaller windows.

"Of course, Grace, whatever room you want. Go ahead and put your things in there," Joy replied.

Grace put her things in the room. She looked around. It seemed as though her mom was anticipating that she would pick that room. It was already emptied, except the bed and a mirror. She took a hard look around the room. *Yeah, this room will be good for me. The windows are pretty high up. Anyone would have a hard time trying to look through them from the outside. Ugh! Why am I thinking this way? There's nothing to be afraid of. Nobody is going to try to look at me. God is with me! God is bigger, and He's already delivered me from Fear. Fear is so persistent. It doesn't matter. I have God. And He will protect me. This room will be good either way.*

Grace walked out and sat at the table near where her mom was cooking. Nothing fancy, just hamburgers, brown gravy, mashed potatoes, and canned green beans. It was a good meal, one of their favorite easy meals. Nobody gave mention to the fact that the boys were leaving soon and were going to be gone for the whole rest of the summer and school year, but they did sit there and try and enjoy each other's company. Bittersweet indeed.

Chapter 12

Lighthouse and Firehouse

That next day was Sunday. The day Grace was looking forward to the most was here. It was the first time in a very long time that Grace stepped inside a church. She was excited about it. Early in the morning, Joy told Grace that she was no longer going to Abundant Life Christian Fellowship but didn't offer an explanation. Grace couldn't help but wonder if it had to do with Jean being allowed to attend a service and still practice witchcraft, or if there was no church discipline regarding what happened. Maybe both. Joy was kind of a church hopper anyway, so maybe it was just her time to move on. Grace was glad either way. Although she had no idea if Jean and her boys were even around anymore, she just wanted to forget about them and be as far away from that family and situation as possible. She didn't hate them; she just didn't want reminders of the trauma she went through. Grace and Joy were now attending a church named Selah House of Worship. Church services used to be hard for Grace to engage in before her time in

Light House

Oregon, but now she wanted to give all her attention to the teachings and worship.

Also, now that Grace was thirteen, she really wanted to join Selah's youth group too. They called Sunday evening youth service *Lighthouse*. Wednesday-night youth meeting was called *Firehouse*. Joy made sure Grace was able to attend all of them regularly.

Since there was a midweek service for the adults, Firehouse went to another room for a less-formal service. Lighthouse, however, was able to use the full sanctuary for Sunday evenings. It didn't take long for Grace to become a faithful attender of Selah's Sunday morning service, Lighthouse, and Firehouse meetings. She loved worshiping with the other youth, learning, growing, and being a part of the corporate worship of the Almighty.

Selah House of Worship also had a private Christian school, Selah Christian School (SCS), and many of the students there also attended the services held by the church side of things. Grace had only been going to the church for three weeks when, after a service, Grace went to join a few girls whom she became friends with. One of them, Natalia, who also went to SCS, invited Grace to go to the SCS graduation coming up that Saturday. The private school year ended much later than the public school counterparts.

"Hey, Grace, are you going to the Selah Christian School graduation?" Natalia asked.

"I don't know anyone graduating," Grace stated. *I'm new here. But she is inviting me, so maybe I should try and go. I'm not invited to that many things, and I want to be Natalia's friend.*

"Oh, it doesn't matter. You can come anyways. You know, support the seniors." Natalia was pretty convincing, and Grace didn't want to let her new friend down.

"When is it?" Grace asked.

"This Saturday, at 7:00 p.m."

"I guess so. I'll have to ask my mom though," Grace finally answered. *This is going to be weird. I don't know anybody. I'll just sit with Natalia if my mom lets me go. She's the one inviting me.*

When Grace's mom, Joy, picked her up, Grace asked if she could go the SCS graduation, and Joy said she could go. *Oh great, now I have to go. I don't know what I'm supposed to do at a graduation.* She had never attended a graduation before and didn't know what to expect, what to wear, etc.

Saturday came, and she remembered that there was a graduation to go to. Grace reminder her mom because she didn't want to seem like a flaky friend who would forget to show up to something she was invited to. When it was time to go, they left so they could show up at least fifteen minutes early. Grace left in what she was already wearing, not really knowing what anyone else would be wearing. She reminded herself, *I'll just sit next to Natalia when I get there.*

Joy just dropped Grace off in the parking lot. Grace approached the sanctuary where they were also holding the ceremony. She felt all alone in the crowd and aimless. Not really sure where she should be exactly. She walked in the back door of the sanctuary about fifteen minutes before it started. Grace looked around. Everyone was dressed nicely, but she just had a pair of jeans, a T-shirt, and some dirty, ugly old tennis shoes on.

*Oh, it's that kind of event. I look so silly. I'm so embarrassed!
Natalia, where is Natalia?* Grace spotted Natalia in the
second to the front row, all filled up already. She was sitting
with her family, facing forward, and didn't see her friend
come in. *Okay, I can't sit with Natalia. I don't see anyone else
I know. Everyone is starting to sit down. It's about to start. Just
find a seat in the back and try to hide. I'm so out of place.*

Grace felt angry that she showed up and that she
didn't dress up better; maybe then she would have felt
she belonged there, or at least could have pretended she
belonged there. She found an open seat in the aisle, the
second to the last row, and sat next to a half wall where the
sound board controls were located and leaned up against
it. She felt uncomfortable and way out of place; she didn't
have a place. *Hopefully I'm hidden enough.*

She looked at the clock behind her. *Ten minutes to
start. I wish it was done already. I wish I didn't even come.
Natalia didn't even notice me coming in, and I'm not about
to walk in front of everyone looking like this to tell her I'm
here. But I'm already here, and my mom is gone. I'm stuck.
Just stay invisible, and maybe nobody will see me. I wish the
graduation would just hurry up and be over with.*

Grace must have been staring off into space; she didn't
see Israel Phillips approach her. He was the drummer for
the youth group, fifteen years old. Previously, Grace asked
Natalia during Lighthouse who he was. Grace thought he
was so very handsome but never was bold enough to go up
and meet him herself. Grace knew his name, but he didn't
know hers.

"Are you okay?" Israel asked as he stopped in that open
aisle directly in front of her.

Grace looked up. Her heart stopped beating, and she must have had a dumb look on her face. *It's Israel, and he's talking to me?* "Uh...yeah... I'm okay," Grace quietly responded. *Did he even hear me?* Grace could feel her ears heat up and knew she was probably turning pink with embarrassment for not answering loud enough and that the boy she thought was so handsome was actually talking to her. She quickly tried to wipe the surprise from her eyes and realized her mouth was open. *Shut your mouth and smile, girl!*

"I'm Israel." He held out his hand to meet her.

"I'm Grace." Grace shook his hand.

Israel leaned in a little closer. "What's your name?"

Great, he couldn't hear me. "I'm Grace." She forced her answer to be a little bit louder. It seemed to go in slow motion as this was a moment where Grace's silly teenage heart fluttered. Grace was flattered that such a handsome boy wanted to meet her, that he even noticed her to begin with. *I must look so dumb and out of place.* But Israel didn't seem to notice what she was wearing; he just wanted to meet her. He had seen her come to youth group but didn't know she was interested in SCS events and activities. Israel also was a student at SCS and was there with his parents, supporting the seniors who graduated. His parents were Edward and Charlotte Phillips.

"Nice to meet you." Israel seemed genuinely happy to meet her.

"Nice to meet you too." Grace's smile just got bigger, and she seemed to forget how uncomfortable she had been.

"I saw you were here by yourself and wanted to see if you were okay and meet you," he tried to explain why he was there with her. He smiled at her, and it made her feel like she belonged, that she mattered, and that she was at the right place at the right time. "Well, graduation is about to start." He looked at the clock and behind him toward the stage. The school staff was getting in place for the ceremony to start.

Someone announced on the microphone, "If you all could find your seats, ladies and gentlemen. We are about to start the ceremony."

"I better go back to my seat. I'll see you later," he whispered. He gave one more awkward smile and widened his eyes, like he was embarrassed himself to be still standing when everyone else pretty much found their seats.

"Of course." Grace smiled big. She found herself staring as he walked back to his parents. *Those eyes and that smile. Quit staring!* Grace realized what she was doing and jolted her head to look toward the stage as the ceremony started. Grace sat up and had a better posture. She was feeling happy and forgot how embarrassed she felt. She tried to look attentive and like she was truly interested in the graduation, but all she could think about was Israel—that he came up to her, he wanted to see if she was okay, that he wanted to meet her, and how handsome he was. Grace was giddy inside. She was never noticed (that she was aware of) by any boy before, especially one so good-looking and a Christian too.

When the graduation finished and everyone was mingling and congratulating the graduated, Grace found her way to her friend Natalia to let her know she made it. Natalia was glad to see her friend but had to leave with her family when they were ready to go, which was right away.

Everyone else had their after graduation parties and plans, so Grace just left and met her mom, who was waiting for her in the parking lot.

When Grace first arrived at that graduation, she felt very angry that she was even there; but when she left, she thought that there was a purpose in it and secretly hoped that meeting Israel had something to do with it.

Grace wasn't normally an outspoken person in the way of being any sort of center of attention. She was normally quiet in volume and preferred one-on-one conversations but also enjoyed belonging to the group. She really did begin to belong to Selah's youth, and it felt good for a change. Although she was quiet in volume, she wasn't shy. Grace quickly made many friends and knew everyone who attended regularly. She learned to make newcomers feel welcomed, knowing how important it was for her when she first started coming. Grace was encouraged to know that other youth had a heart for God like she did.

Worship during all services were dynamic. Grace believed that, each time, God was present, that He inhabited their praises and was with them when they gathered. Knowing all that God had done for her, she openly and willfully expressed her thanksgiving in song and stayed eager to hear the teachings to help build the foundation for her beliefs. A common prompting from the pulpit was that Christians should be reading the Bible on their own. There it was, again and again. She faced it weekly and was reminded how important it was for her to know the Bible for herself so she could *know God*. She grew in knowledge and in wisdom and started reading the Bible every day.

Sometimes just a few verses, but she made sure she was reading. It was like she was supernaturally enabled to read and understand when it came to the Bible, whereas before reading anything was a huge struggle.

Chapter 13

Fear Desperate to Come Back

It was a warm summer night. When Grace was trying to sleep, a pack of something strange started to howl and squeal from outside her window. The sound startled her. Her heart started to race, and her mind started swirling again with thoughts. She lifted her head off her pillow and turned facing outward to help her hear more clearly. *What in the world? That sounds like demons and devils. If demons made noise, that's what they would sound like, I'm sure!* Those were awful, ugly noises that she had never heard before. Grace closed her eyes and tried to shake it off, knowing in the back of her mind that it was probably some kind of animal pack. Since her heart was so jolted, it commenced to pound harder. Soon that was all she could hear: the pounding of her own heart. *Everything's fine. It's just animals.*

Not another moment later, visions bombarded her in her room—thousands of wicked faces, demons, and goblins. Both horrific and gory faces surrounded her. No bodies, just faces that filled her room, sneering, gnashing their teeth, and taunting Grace. The faces came close, rushing toward her

and back again, taking turns, showing off their individual ugliness. It was like a contest to see which one would scare Grace the most. This was not something that Grace had ever seen or imagined in her life. She could not stay quiet about it and spoke in a whisper, with a quiet authority in prayer, "In the name of Jesus, I cast you all out of my room. Get out now in the name of Jesus. Flee! Go!" Suddenly they disappeared as quickly as they came; the sounds of the creatures outside ceased with it. With that, Grace was reminded again that God was still with her, and God was bigger. She had peace as she was able to turn around to sleep soundly. Another victory.

The next morning, she talked with her mom. "Hey, Mom, did you hear those noises last night? It sounded crazy."

"Yes, I heard it too. It must have been a pack of javelinas around."

"Are you serious? They sounded like demons or something. It was ugly…javelinas? Wow, those were some crazy noises they made," Grace said. *Glad it wasn't my imagination. They sounded like the devils I saw in spirit.* Grace shook her head as she remembered what happened the night before and rolled her eyes at Fear's sorry attempts.

This was one of Fear's last attempts to rule over Grace. He kept his distance but didn't forget how he ruled her once. He would lurk at a distance all throughout the rest of Grace's life, waiting for an opportune time that he could get close—still clinging to any hope that she could, or would, become afraid again for him to control her once more.

However, for years, Grace was left alone. If there ever were any sign of Fear's presence, Grace's prayers would instantly demolish any such being.

Chapter 14

A Prophet Speaks to Grace

For the duration of the summer, Grace joined her mom at her work, which was cleaning houses. She made a few dollars here and there for her own spending money to use for whatever she wanted. Many times, Grace would give the money to the church in offering. Joy was always giving and generous. Grace was influenced by that. Money was always coming in and out of their hands as they were open to opportunities to give. Sometimes she would use her money to buy her own food after youth fellowship.

After youth meetings, everyone was invited to hang out or fellowship. Those times fostered close relationships among the youth. Sometimes the hangout was at somebody's house but mainly at a favorite restaurant. If Grace could get a ride, then she usually went with them; if not, then she just went home with her mom when she came to pick her up. This was so, even when eighth grade school started. Her relationships with some of the youth kids became stronger and more closely knit together; some would become lifetime friends.

It was August 1. Eighth grade had started. Grace walked around with a quiet confidence. She had learned how to make friends and be more outgoing, even though she was still quiet in volume. She sought out especially those whom she thought might be all alone or didn't have many or any friends. She talked openly about her faith and found some friends who believed the same as her; others did not.

Grace believed that each Christian has a calling and purpose that is God-given, maybe a task or mission of sorts, but she didn't know her specific purpose. She was thirteen, still under the care and provisions of her parents, so she didn't concern herself trying to figure it all out. She did know, however, that there was a general way to live as a Christian: to act like a body, one in purpose; to share in other Christians' burdens; and to share in their joys—cutting the burdens in half and doubling in the joys. There was the Great Commission from the Gospel of Matthew 28 directed by Jesus to all His followers to go and share the salvation message to those near and to those around the world and being a part of it in some way. Also try and live to please God. Grace interpreted that as to not sin. That's what Grace focused on for the time being, just to be good and pleasing to God in thought, actions, and words, and be open to sharing with those around her.

Just a couple months after school started, on October 3, 1998, Joy took Grace to an evangelical tent meeting. The main speaker was Brock McDowell. The large tent was located in a back street off from the main business street in one of the smaller church parking lots there. There was tarp on the ground to cover the dirt and concrete, a makeshift stage with a microphone, and many fold-up chairs in a few columns and rows. There were about thirty people in attendance. The service started off with singing, praying, and reading some scripture. The main purpose of the meeting was to "give prophetic words" to some of the people who showed up. Joy, still intrigued by personal prophesies and knowing the future (especially prophetically) was always drawn to meetings like this, always hoping to get a "word" for herself, or her family. Joy went to meetings of this sort at every local opportunity. Grace didn't really know what she thought about somebody claiming to be prophetic. She had been reading the prophets of the Bible, and her favorite, Joseph who was the one with the coat of many colors. Grace knew prophets in the Bible were people who gave God's Words to the people, or showed them future events. *Are prophets for today? Is this Brock McDowell really hearing from God?* Grace didn't know. She sat in the meeting, and listened. Brock started to call on people and told them a message he claimed he was hearing from God to give to those individuals. None of the words sounded bad, or necessarily wrong. She just observed.

All of a sudden, Brock pointed at Grace. "This young lady right here."

Grace made eye contact with Brock as he continued to speak.

"Young lady, the Lord loves you, and you got a special place with God. And God, in the Spirit, is just going to build a wall of fire around you. You love God, and the Lord is going to put a wall of fire around you, and the devil won't be able to touch you. God is preserving your life because He has a purpose and plan for your life. The Lord told me that He's going to give you a hunger for spiritual things like you've never had before. You're going to find yourself having some unusual dreams. In the dreams, whatever they are, the ones that you will know are from God is because His presence is not only going to be in the dream; but when you wake up, His presence is going to be in your room. You're going to know that it's a message from God. God is going to give you the interpretation of the dreams. You just might as well start getting happy and shake off the blues and shake off all the things that you wish could have been different. Things are going to get good for you, but you just stay close to Jesus."

That was it—then he moved on to speaking to somebody else.

Shake off the blues? I'm not sad. Who knows. I'm not taking any of this as gospel. But you never know. I've seen spiritual things before in vision. Not in a good way, but it was like seeing visions, like those demon heads. I'd much rather see visions from God though, not the enemy. Put it on the shelf. If it happens—great, it happens. If not, it must not be God telling me these things. The main thing to ask is, Is it biblical? The Bible does talk about young men seeing visions and old dreaming dreams. But I'm young. Those are spiritual gifts from God. Grace thought as she recalled Acts 2:16–17 (ESV):

> But this is what was uttered through the
>   prophet Joel:
> And in the last days it shall be, God declares,
> that I will pour out my Spirit on all flesh,
> and your sons and your daughters shall
>   prophesy,
> and your young men shall see visions,
> and your old men shall dream dreams.

Who really knows the future but God? Grace didn't know this till well into her own future, that Brock's words from God would speak into her life, even decades later. They would come about at just the right time as a testament to God's greatness and faithfulness to accomplish what He ordains and purposes according to His will. Thirteen-year-old Grace pondered those words and kept them stored in her heart and mind and even wrote them down in a new journal she got. She would be able to recall them again and again, which would become an anchor of hope for difficult times ahead.

After the meeting, Joy was offered a cassette-tape recording of the prophecies given to Grace, and she took it.

Dear Lord, may Your will be done on earth as it is in heaven. Whatever you want for my life, I will accept it.

Chapter 15

A Look Back

Grace was born in Sierra Vista, Arizona. She and her siblings grew up there until Grace turned three. At age three, the whole family moved to Bend, Oregon, where Gramma and Grampa Moor lived. They lived in a three-story home that Gramma and Grampa owned. After Grace's fourth birthday, they moved back to Sierra Vista, Arizona, which was also where Joy's parents lived. The Jensens stayed there until the end of Grace's second grade, and during that summer, they moved back to Central Oregon. While they were there, they moved a couple times. In Oregon, they lived in Sunriver, Alfalfa, and then Bend for Grace's third through fifth grade school years. For third and fourth grade, she went to the same school, but in fifth grade, she was transferred to another school when they moved. When sixth grade came, they were all back in Sierra Vista, Arizona. Then it was in seventh grade where this story, *Grace over Fear*, began. Up until that point, Grace had moved several times and had been to five different schools and had attended many different churches.

From the time Grace was born and up until age twelve (and beyond), Grace was exposed to the Christian church. Her mother took her faithfully, whether her parents were together, separated, or divorced. Grace, as a child, attended children's church and was exposed to the elementary teachings of the Bible. Bible teachings from children's church kept a consistency in Grace's learning about God. Even if they went to many different churches, the Bible never changed. Grace doesn't ever remember not believing the Bible; she just remembers the day she came to know God instead of just knowing about Him.

When Fear bombarded Grace's life at the tender age of twelve, it was all a part of God's plan. He used the depraved things of this world to reveal the gloriousness of His salvation. The gloriousness to bring Grace unto Himself, revealing His power, His divine will and purpose, to become Grace's all in all, her salvation and source. In God's infinite wisdom, all she went through was ultimately God's provision in order to bring about the purposes of God. These are principles of God's sovereignty in all heaven and earth.

It was as a painted picture. A picture of contrasts. The deepest darkness had to be painted first as a backdrop in Grace's life in order that when the brightest, most brilliant light of God came, it would be revealed in all God's glory and power—the power of God unto salvation, the most important event in the life of the believer. This picture of Grace's life, though the experience was not fun for Grace, was revealed that it was for the purpose of her salvation. Grace understood that even though Satan—through Fear, witches, and warlocks—meant it for destruction (to steal, kill, and destroy her), it changed the course of her destiny on earth and for all eternity for the good and for her spiritual good. Grace was within God's purpose and plan all along.

Grace over Fear.

DER THE LAW,

out the shedding of blood there is no forgiveness of sins.

But now under *Grace*

st has entered into heaven itself appearing before God on our behalf,

not to be repeatedly sacrificed, but has appeared once and for all

to put away sin by the blood sacrifice of himself.

Not only dealing with sin, but to save those who are eagerly waiting for him.

~ Hebrews 9 : 22 - 28

About the Author

Bethany L. Correia is first and foremost a Christian, a wife, and a mother to a perfectly blended family of ten children. She's currently a homemaker and homeschools her two youngest children in Central Texas.

She completed some courses at Cochise College, a community campus where she grew up. She intended on becoming an educator. After her firstborn came, she stopped attending college to attend to her new family. Her energies were spent on being a wife and mother at home. No regrets.

About a decade later, she transferred credits to the Art Institute of Pittsburgh online division to become an interior designer. It consumed much time, so she put it on hold again for her family. Regardless of her schooling, Bethany believes the education pursuit did not cease but rather presented beautiful opportunities within the realms of homeschooling her own children. Both teaching and artistic design have become major parts of Bethany's personal life and expression.

Bethany has always written through journaling and note-taking. This has helped her process life, spirituality, and education. She finds writing to be a great outlet and continues in it for personal endeavors. Since it naturally flows for her, writing Grace Over Fear has come about. She hopes that this is the beginning of many more books. Her prayer is that anything she writes and publishes will be to and for the glory of the One God who has written her story. "In your book were written, every one of them, the days that were formed for me, when as yet there was none of them" (Psalm 139:16, ESV).